'ULA LI'I and the MAGIC SHARK

By Donivee Martin Laird

Illustrated by Carol Jossem

Barnaby Books   Honolulu, Hawaii

Also By Barnaby Books:

The Three Little Hawaiian Pigs and the Magic Shark
Keaka and the Liliko'i Vine
Wili Wai Kula and the Three Mongooses

First published in Honolulu, Hawaii by:

Barnaby Books—a partnership

3290 Pacific Heights Road

Honolulu, Hawaii 96813

Printed and bound in Hong Kong under the

direction of:

Mandarin Offset Marketing (H.K.) Ltd.

Library of Congress Catalogue Number 86-3390

ISBN 0-940350-09-2

TO OUR GOOD FRIEND BARNABY

PRONUNCIATION GUIDE

The 12 letters in the Hawaiian alphabet are:
A, E, H, I, K, L, M, N, O, P, U, W

consonants
H, K, L, M, N, P are pronounced as in English
W is usually pronounced as V

vowels
A like a in farm
E like e in set
I like y in pretty

O like o in hold
U like oo in soon

plural
As there is no S in Hawaiian, the plural is formed by word usage or the addition of another word such as nā to the sentence.

The Magic Shark had been in the dump, where the Three Little Hawaiian Pigs had thrown him, for several weeks. He was hot, hungry, and very anxious to get back into the water.

Then, one warm, sticky Saturday two children were scurrying around looking for treasures. They found the flat, rolled up shark. "Look," said the little girl. "It's a perfectly good beach mat."

"Keep it," said the boy. "Papa says we are going to the beach for a swim as soon as he is pau dumping the lichee branches."

The Magic Shark couldn't believe his ears. They were going to the beach and taking him along. With a thump he was tossed into the back of a pickup truck. The boy and his sister climbed in and sat on top of him. (The shark didn't like that one bit.)

After what seemed like endless bouncing and jolting down a dusty road, the truck stopped.

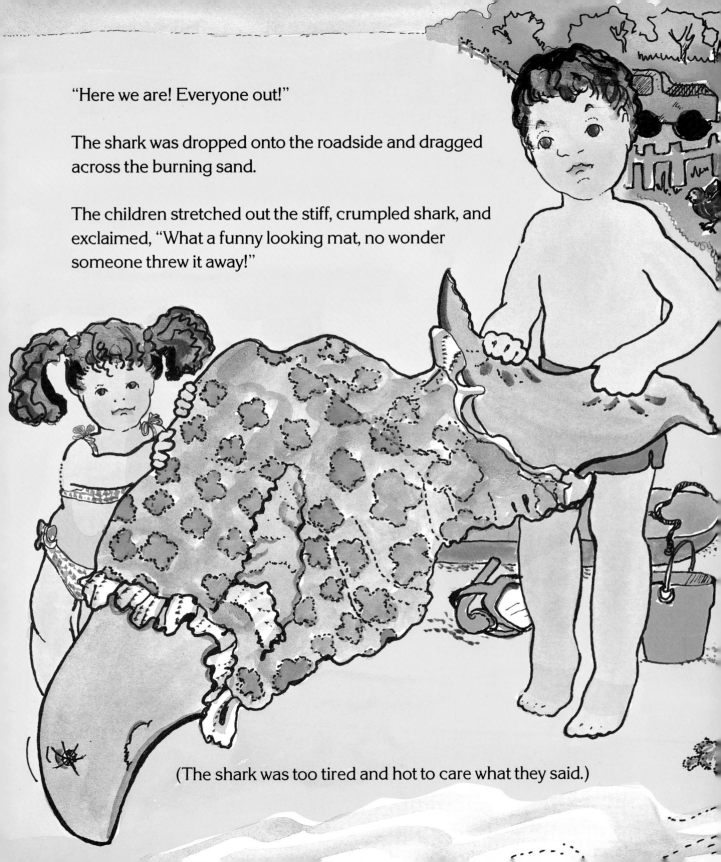

"Here we are! Everyone out!"

The shark was dropped onto the roadside and dragged across the burning sand.

The children stretched out the stiff, crumpled shark, and exclaimed, "What a funny looking mat, no wonder someone threw it away!"

(The shark was too tired and hot to care what they said.)

The Magic Shark could hear the ocean, see the ocean, and smell the ocean, but he was too far away to feel its coolness. Enviously, he watched the girl and boy leap into the water.

Over and over again, the waves washed up the sand towards him and then whooshed back into the bay without him.

Finally, a giant wave curled across the bay. It crashed at the edge of the beach and rushed quickly up the sand. Over the shark it gurgled and foamed, pulling him towards the sea.

The instant the water touched the shark, air rushed into his body again. With a flick of his tail, he joined the wave and once more the Magic Shark was free.

It wasn't long until the shark realized that although he was cool, wet, and free, he still had a big problem. He was hungry. He put on one of his many disguises and went ashore to cruise around.

Wearing a pair of faded blue jeans and a cut off tee shirt, the Magic Shark rode his skateboard down a wide, smooth street.

"'Ula Li'i, come take this food to Puna," called a voice.

"Food!" thought the shark as he leaped off of his skateboard and peeked through a hibiscus hedge. He saw a woman talking to a little girl.

"Puna has a bad cold," the woman was saying. "Here is some poke, kūlolo, and a nice piece of kālua pig. Please take them to her. Stay on the main road and go around the hau tree forest. Don't take any short cuts or stop to talk to strangers. Do you understand?"

"Yes, mama," replied the little girl taking the lauhala basket and smiling sweetly at her mother.

"Kālua Pig! Kūlolo! Poke!" The shark was thrilled at such wonderful news. These were his absolute favorite treats and there they were all ready for him to eat. All he had to do was take them away from one little girl. "Hikiwawe! Easily done!" exclaimed the excited shark.

ʻUla Liʻi trotted off carrying the basket of food to her tūtū.

Meanwhile, the Magic Shark dashed through a short cut in the hau trees. He planned to wait down the road and play one of his tricks in order to get the basket of food.

Using his very best magic, the shark set up a malasada wagon and dressed himself as the cook. Just as he was hanging out his sign, 'Ula Li'i came into view.

"Fresh, hot malasadas. Terrific for a kupuna with a cold," he called as 'Ula Li'i walked by. She paused. "Bargain today only, 35 cents one, 50 cents two," said the shark smiling.

'Ula Li'i thought for a moment. She remembered that her mother had told her not to talk to strangers and to take the food straight to Puna. "No, this food is for Puna." She shook her head and walked away.

"I'll trade you three fat malasadas for your basket."
'Ula Li'i kept on walking.

Now the Magic Shark wasn't one to give up easily, so he raced down another short cut through the hau trees.

Pretty soon, along came 'Ula Li'i, skipping and singing. She stopped when she saw what was beside the road. The shark, wearing his favorite disguise, was holding a tray of colorful, sweet shave ice.

"Shave ice today?" asked the kind shave ice man. ('Ula Li'i didn't know it was the Magic Shark.)

"I don't have money," said 'Ula Li'i sadly. She was a bit warm after all of her walking and the shave ice looked so 'ono.

"Are you sure?" wondered the shave ice man nicely. "Those are deep pockets in your skirt. Perhaps there is a little bit in the bottom of one of them."

'Ula Li'i looked down at her skirt. "Perhaps," she said quietly.

"Why don't you look?" asked the Magic Shark with a friendly smile. "Here, hand me your basket, I will hold it while you check."

Just as 'Ula Li'i was about to hand her basket to the Magic Shark, she once again remembered her mother's instructions. "Oh, no!" she exclaimed. "Mother will be huhū if I disobey her."

Off she ran, leaving the shark with his mouth open in surprise. He had been so sure he would get the basket that time.

The shark wasn't ready to give up yet. He had one more idea to try. He took still another short cut and ran ahead of ʻUla Liʻi to Puna's house. When he got there, he dressed himself as a paper boy.

"Puna," he called through the screen door. "It's me, your paper boy."

"There is a big ʻōpelu sale at the fish market. It is right here in the paper."

There was nothing Puna loved better than 'ōpelu, and a sale on her favorite fish was too much for her to resist. Forgetting how miserable she felt with her cold, she threw on her mu'umu'u and hat and dashed out the door.

(She was in such a hurry she didn't even stop to check the paper herself.)

As soon as Puna was gone, the Magic Shark slipped out from behind a large gardenia bush. He jumped up the front stairs and carefully stepped into Puna's house. After cautiously checking to see that no one else was there, he changed into Puna's nightgown, putting a grey wig and a frilly nightcap on his head.

Just as the shark was getting settled in bed, ʻUla Liʻi knocked at the door. "Puna, it is ʻUla Liʻi," she called. "I have something ʻono for you in my basket."

"Oh, come in my Darling Moʻopuna," called the shark trying to sound like Puna and trying not to sound too excited. (He knew he had the kālua pig, kūlolo, and poke this time!) ʻUla Liʻi was happy to hear her tūtū sounding better so she entered the house smiling cheerfully.

"Why Puna," said 'Ula Li'i as she approached the bed. "I never noticed what big pepeiao you have."

"Ah, my little Musubi, all the better to hear you with," answered the shark reaching for the basket.

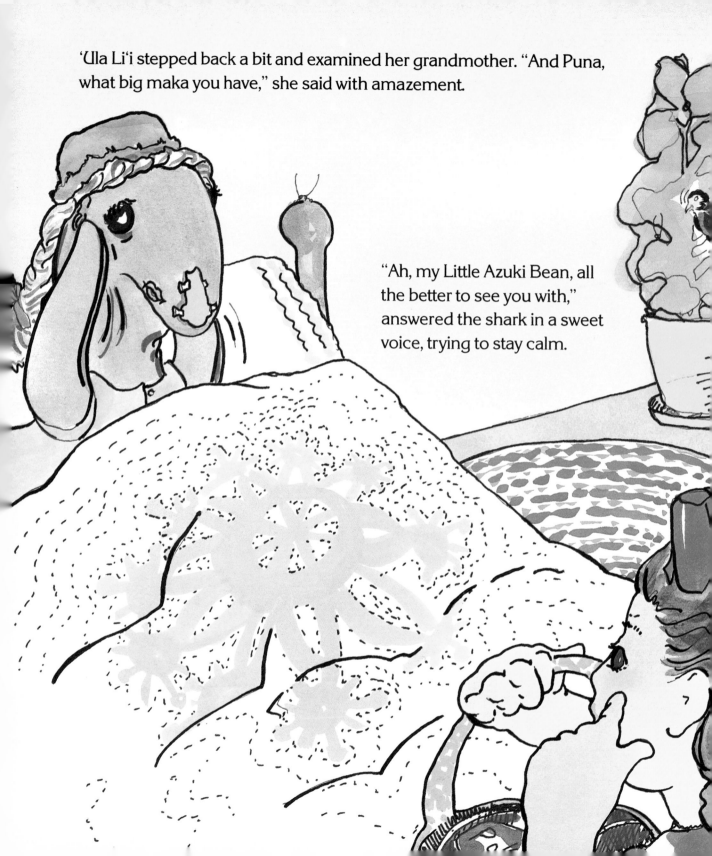

'Ula Li'i stepped back a bit and examined her grandmother. "And Puna, what big maka you have," she said with amazement.

"Ah, my Little Azuki Bean, all the better to see you with," answered the shark in a sweet voice, trying to stay calm.

"But Puna," stammered a confused 'Ula Li'i.
"Your ihu, it too is so big."

"Ah, my Little Mooncake, all the better to smell with," said the shark quickly,
trying to reach the basket. He was getting very impatient.

'Ula Li'i looked carefully at her kupuna and frowned. Then she shook her head and said, "Puna, what a very big waha you have."

This was too much for the Magic Shark. "Ah, my Little Sweet Potato, all the better to eat your kālua pig, kūlolo, and poke with," he shouted as he jumped out of bed.

'Ula Li'i shrieked and ran across the room.
"Give me that basket!" said the Magic Shark in his most angry voice.

"No!" said 'Ula Li'i. "I will
scream." And she did. And
very loudly, too.

Working in the cane field next to Puna's house there was a hanawai man cleaning rubbish out of the irrigation ditches. When he heard 'Ula Li'i scream, he ran to the house and pushed open the door.

He saw 'Ula Li'i cornered by the shark. The shark was just about to grab her basket of food.

"Stop!" yelled the hanawai man as he ran forward. He grabbed the shark. "I'll take care of you," he said.

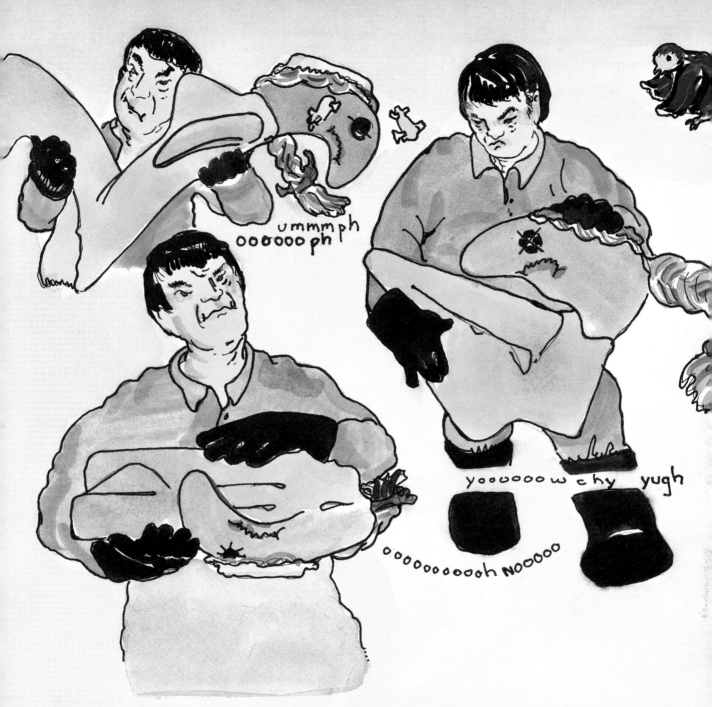

With cracks and snaps and loud shark yells, the hanawai man slowly began to fold the Magic Shark. Over and over he folded the shark just like the pieces of sugar cane that were fished out of the ditches.

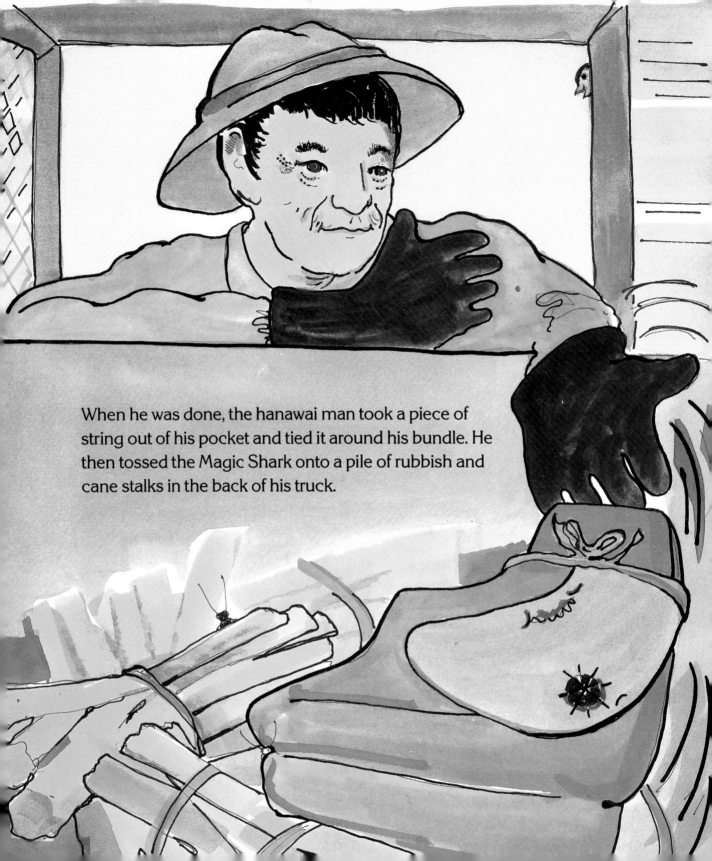

When he was done, the hanawai man took a piece of string out of his pocket and tied it around his bundle. He then tossed the Magic Shark onto a pile of rubbish and cane stalks in the back of his truck.

About this time, Puna came home. She was upset that there wasn't a sale on 'ōpelu, but had bought two fish anyway.

When she heard about what had happened, she was so happy that 'Ula Li'i was safe, she gave the hanawai man both of her 'ōpelu and a piece of kūlolo as a mahalo.

Then Puna sent 'Ula Li'i straight home (reminding her not to take short cuts and to stay away from strangers) and climbed back into her bed.

When the pau hana whistle blew at the sugar mill several hours later, ʻUla Liʻi was safe at home with her mother, Puna was having a snack of kālua pig, and the hanawai man was tying string around one final bundle of sticks.

He then gathered the last bits of cane stalks, leaves, and other litter. They were thrown into his truck with the rest of the trash (don't forget the Magic Shark) and the hanawai man was nearly pau for the day.

Down a certain dusty road the hanawai man drove. The cane stalks, twigs, and Magic Shark bounced and jolted endlessly as the truck bumped along.

DUMP

Finally the truck stopped and the hanawai man climbed onto his pile of rubbish (and one angry shark). He worked quickly, thinking about the hot furo and tasty ʻōpelu supper that waited for him at home. One by one he tossed the bundles of trash (and a very upset Magic Shark) into the dump.

The bundles of trash and the twisted, folded shark
bounced over the top of an old rusty car,
rolled down a pile of garbage,
and finally came to rest
inside a box of overripe papayas.
The Magic Shark
was very angry
at himself.

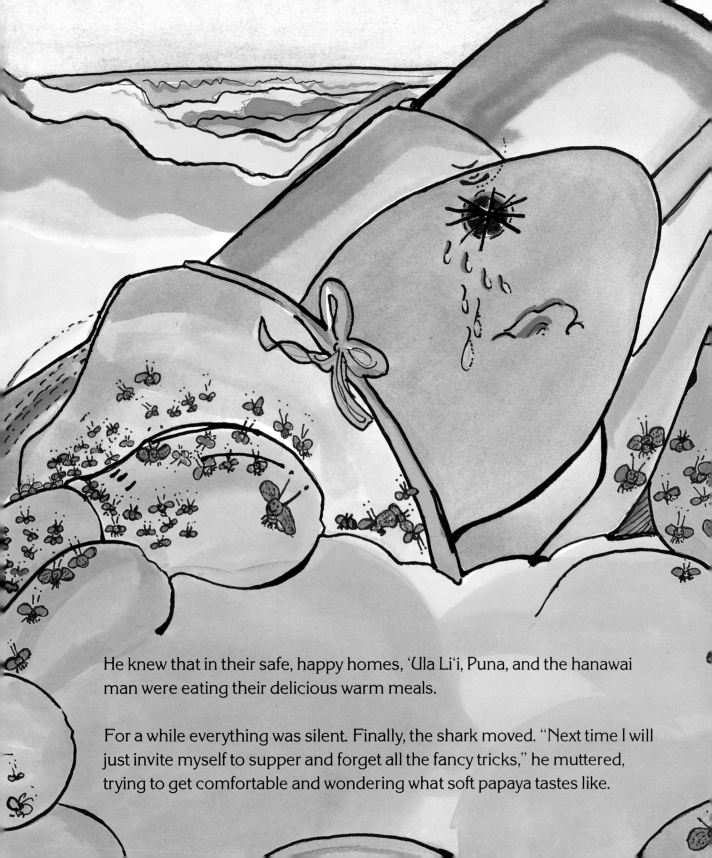

He knew that in their safe, happy homes, ʻUla Liʻi, Puna, and the hanawai man were eating their delicious warm meals.

For a while everything was silent. Finally, the shark moved. "Next time I will just invite myself to supper and forget all the fancy tricks," he muttered, trying to get comfortable and wondering what soft papaya tastes like.

GLOSSARY

'ULA LI'I   *Li'i* means little and *'ula* means red.
                 'Ula Li'i is little red.

KUPUNA   A Hawaiian word meaning grandparent.
PUNA   A shortened form of *Kupuna*.
TŪTŪ   Hawaiian for grandmother.

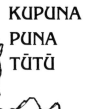

MO'OPUNA   A word meaning grandchild.

LAUHALA   The leaf of the pandanus which is used in weaving baskets, hats, and rugs.

HIBISCUS   The state flower of Hawaii. A popular flower used in hedges or alone as a small tree or bush.

POKE   A Hawaiian way of preparing raw fish. Usually seaweed, soy sauce, green onions, and hot chili peppers are mixed with chunks of raw fish. *Poke* means to slice or cut into crosswise pieces.

KŪLOLO   Pudding made of baked or steamed grated taro and coconut milk.

KĀLUA PIG — Pig that has been baked in an underground oven or imu.

'ONO — Hawaiian word for delicious.

HAU TREE — A many branched tree that is a relative of the hibiscus. It can grow to heights of 12 feet and spread across the ground in thickets that form a dense network of trunks and branches.

HIKIWAWE — A word meaning quickly, speedily, or possible to do quickly.

SHAVE ICE — Powdery ice shavings served in a paper cone and covered with sweet, flavored syrup.

MALASADA — A tasty, sugary, fried Portuguese treat that resembles a large round piece of doughnut.

HUHŪ A word meaning angry.

MUʻUMUʻU A long, loose fitting woman's dress.

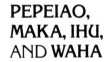

ʻŌPELU A type of mackerel.

PEPEIAO, MAKA, IHU, AND WAHA Hawaiian words meaning ears, eyes, nose and mouth (in that order).

MUSUBI A Japanese word for rice formed into a firm ball or triangle.

AZUKI BEAN A sweet bean used in cooking Japanese food.

MOONCAKE A brown, sweet, heavy pastry eaten especially during the Chinese Moon Festival, which usually falls in the month of August.

MAHALO Hawaiian word for thank you.

HANAWAI

Hana means to work, *wai* means water. Together they mean to irrigate. The *hanawai* men on the sugar plantations had the job of keeping the irrigation ditches free of debris and running smoothly.

PAU HANA

Pau means finished and *hana* means work; *pau hana* time is the end of the work day. On the sugar plantations it is signaled by a blast of the mill whistle.

FURO

Japanese equivalent of a hot tub.

PAPAYA

Native of tropical America and favorite fruit in Hawaii. The trees are 5 to 25 feet tall with thin trunks and a crown of sturdy branches and large green leaves.

PAU

A Hawaiian word for finished, all done, the end.